Once upon a time there were four little   Rabbits,   and their names were –

Flopsy, Mopsy, Cotton-tail, and Peter. They lived with

their Mother in a sand-bank,

underneath the root of a

very big fir-   ·   tree.

'Now, my dears,' said old

Mrs. Rabbit one morning,

'you may go into the fields or down the lane, but don't

go into Mr. McGregor's garden: your Father had an

accident there; he was put in a

pie   by Mrs. McGregor.

Now run along, and don't get

into mischief. I am going out.'

Then old Mrs. Rabbit took a   basket   and her

umbrella,   and went through the wood to the baker's.

And rushed into the tool-shed,

and jumped into a   can.

It would have been a beautiful

thing to hide in, if it had not

had so much   water   in it.

        Mr. McGregor was quite sure

that Peter was somewhere in the tool-shed, perhaps

hidden underneath a   flower-pot.

He began to turn them over carefully, looking under each.

Presently Peter sneezed –'Kertyschoo!' Mr. McGregor was

after him in no time and tried

to put his foot upon Peter,

who jumped out of a window,

upsetting three plants. The

window was too small for

Mr. McGregor, and he was

the way back to the gate. He lost

one of his shoes among the

cabbages, and the other shoe

amongst the potatoes.

After losing them,

he ran on four legs and

went faster, so that I think he might have got away

altogether if he had not unfortunately run into a

gooseberry net, and got caught by the large buttons on his jacket.

Mr. McGregor came up with a sieve, which he intended to pop upon the top of Peter; but Peter wriggled out just in time, leaving his jacket behind him.

tired of running after Peter. He went back to his work.

After a time Peter began to wander about, going

lippity-lippity – not very fast, and looking all round.

He found a   door   in a   wall;

but it was locked, and there was no

room for a fat little rabbit to squeeze

underneath. An old   mouse   was

running in and out over the stone doorstep, carrying

peas and beans to her family in the wood. Peter asked

her the way to the   gate,   but she had such a large

pea   in her mouth that she could not

answer. She only shook her head at him.

Then he tried to find his way straight across the garden,

but he became more and more puzzled. Presently, he

came to a   pond   where Mr. McGregor filled his

water-cans.

A white   cat   was staring at some   gold-fish,

she sat very, very still,

but now and then the

tip of her tail twitched

as if it were alive. Peter

thought it best to go

away without speaking

to her.

He went back towards the tool-shed, but suddenly, quite close to him, he heard the noise of a hoe – scr-r-ritch, scratch, scratch, scritch. Peter scuttered underneath the bushes. But presently, as nothing happened, he came out, and climbed upon a wheelbarrow and peeped over. The first thing he saw was Mr. McGregor hoeing onions. His back was turned towards Peter, and beyond him was the gate!

Peter got down very quietly off the   wheelbarrow, and started running as fast as he could go. Mr. McGregor caught sight of him at the corner, but  Peter did not care. He slipped underneath the   gate, and was safe at last in the wood outside the garden.

Mr. McGregor hung up the little jacket and the shoes for a   scare-crow   to frighten the blackbirds. Peter never stopped running till he got home to the big fir-   tree.

He was so tired that he flopped down upon the nice soft sand on the floor of the rabbit-hole and shut his eyes. His mother wondered what he had done with his clothes. It was the second little jacket and pair of shoes that Peter had lost in a fortnight!

I am sorry to say that Peter was not very well during the evening. His mother put him to bed, and made some camomile tea; and she gave a dose of it to Peter!

Flopsy, Mopsy, and Cotton-tail, who were good little

bunnies, went down the lane to gather   blackberries:

but Peter, who was very naughty, ran straight away

to Mr. McGregor's garden, and squeezed under

the   gate!

   First he ate some lettuces and some French beans; and

then he ate some   radishes;   and then, feeling rather

sick, he went to look for some parsley.

But round the end of a cucumber frame, whom should

he meet but Mr. McGregor!

Mr. McGregor was on his

hands   and knees planting

out young   cabbages,   but he jumped up and

ran after Peter, waving a   rake   and calling out,

'Stop thief!' Peter was most dreadfully frightened; he

rushed all over the garden, for he had forgotten

Grandma's in the Garbage

written by
Steve and Mica Westover

illustrated by
Mica Westover

Published by Missouri Star Quilt Company

Missouri Star Quilt Company
114 N Davis
Hamilton, Mo. 64644
888-571-1122
info@missouriquiltco.com
Published and Printed in the USA

Cenveo Publisher Services
2901 Byrdhill Road
Richmond, VA 23228

First published in the United States of America by Missouri Star Quilt Company 2015.
Grandma's in the Garbage / written by Steve and Mica Westover, illustrated by Mica Westover
Summary: Grandma creates a memory quilt for her granddaughter from scraps of
unforgettable fabrics.

ISBN - 978-1-63224-011-8

For information regarding the CPSIA on this printed material call:
203-595-3636 and provide reference # LANC – 639242

For our remarkable children
who remind us every day why they are
our treasures.

———— *special thanks* ————

Natalie, Sarah, and Jenny

Thank you for your encouragement and
helping to make a dream come true.

Grandma, why are you digging that dress out of the garbage? **YUCK!**

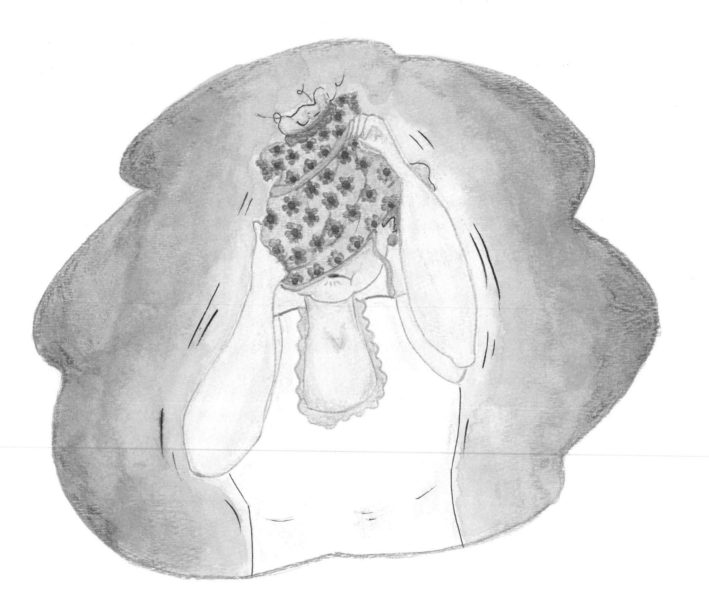

Strange. Why would there be treasure in the trash? That dress will **NEVER** fit her!

Hmmm. I wonder how long she has been doing this?

I wonder if she's going through other people's garbage?

Oh no! What would the neighbors think if they saw
Grandma snooping for treasure in their trash?

She could get in **HUGE** trouble!

I don't want Grandma to go to jail. I would be so sad if she went away for a long time.

Girl Pleads For Grandma's Releas...

MSQC Teaches Students to Quilt

GER goes to... ger Dive

12 Year Old Win County Quilting

...AL DISPLAYS ...N HISTORY

Governor Visits Hamilton

Declares Hamilton, MO Quilt Town, U.S.

was searching for she simply replied, "Treasures." Concerned about the woman's unusual behavior, Detective Scanlan booked her into the City hold...

Late Saturday night, Hamilton City Police arrested an elderly woman digging through her neighbor's garbage. When asked what she was searching for she simply replied, "Treasures." Concerned about the woman's unusual behavior, Detective Scanlan booked her into the City holding overnight. Early the next morning family arrived to bail the woman out. Her granddaughter said, "I don't want Grandma to go to jail. I'd do everything in my power to save her." Impressed by the girl's love for her grandma, police released the woman on condition that she will no longer dig through other people's trash. She is, however, permitted to dig through her own trash, though it isn't recommended.

I must save her from a life of crime!

"Grandma, **STOP EVERYTHING!** We need to talk." "You will **NOT** find treasure in our garbage and you will not find it in our neighbors garbage either."

Grandma laughed, "I'm not digging in the trash!
These old clothes aren't garbage at all. They are special
because they remind me of you."

18

"This dress reminds me of you
as an itty, bitty baby. So precious."

"You took this blankie everywhere you went."

"You even took it
swimming."

"I remember this tie! Daddy wore it
when I was sick. He took care of me!"

"Your mother's apron reminds me that your mom will do anything to take care of you."

"I remember when we made monster cookies with sprinkles on them!"

"Grandma, this is for you.
You can have my treasure."

Thank you, dear!
I have something for you too. . .

"I made this special memory quilt as a
treasure just for you."

"Whoa...it's beautiful! Look...I see daddy's tie, and there's my blankie. That's mom's apron, and my baby dress! **I LOVE IT!**"

I love you, sweetie. You are my treasure
and I want you to always remember.

THE END